This Walker book belongs to:

Simon James is an award-winning author and illustrator of books for children
and is a regular speaker in schools and at festivals across the UK and the US.
His books include *Dear Greenpeace, Leon and Bob, Sally and the Limpet,
The Day Jake Vacuumed* and the bestselling Baby Brains series.
Simon likes to draw with a dip pen and uses watercolour paints
for his illustrations. To find out more about Simon James
and his books, visit www.simonjamesbooks.com

First published 2011 by Walker Books Ltd, 87 Vauxhall Walk, London SE11 5HJ

This edition published 2012

2 4 6 8 10 9 7 5 3 1

© 2011 Simon James

This book has been typeset in Goudy

Printed in China

British Library Cataloguing in Publication Data:
a catalogue record for this book is available from the British Library

ISBN 978-1-4063-3842-3

www.walker.co.uk

WALKER BOOKS
AND SUBSIDIARIES

LONDON • BOSTON • SYDNEY • AUCKLAND

Simon James

George Flies South

The leaves on the
trees were turning brown.
Winter was coming.

Lots of birds were heading south.

It was time for George to learn to fly.

"Are you ready, George?" said his mum.

"Not quite," said
George.
"I might fall."

"I think I like my nest best."

"Will you get some worms, Mum?"

"I'll stay here."

Whilst George waited, a strong gust of wind
swept through the park.
It tore through the branches
scattering the leaves everywhere.

George's nest wobbled ...

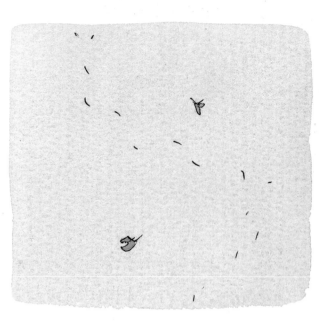

and lifted
into the air.

"Mum," said
George. "Mum,
look at me!"

"I'm flying!

Wheee!"

But George's mum was too far away.

She couldn't hear him calling.

When she flew back, George and his nest were gone!

"George! George!" she cried. "Where are you?"

"I'm here, Mum!" called George. "I flew down in my nest!"

Then, without warning,

George and his nest were on the move again.

"Am I going
south, Mum?"
asked George.

"Hold on!" shouted his mum. "I'm coming!"

But George couldn't hold on

and took off into the air.

"Look at me, Mum!

Look at me!" said George.

"I'm flying again!"

"You can't stay here, George," said his mum.

"You've got to leave your nest. Try to flap your wings!"

George tried.

"Try harder!"

"What are we going to do, Mum?"

Much later the boat stopped. George was lifted

up, up, up into the air.

"Don't move,
George!"
said his mum.

George looked down.

He was glad he still had his nest.

"Don't worry," said his mum. "We'll try again tomorrow."

George curled up and fell fast asleep.

The next morning George woke with a start.

"Look out, George!"

shouted his mum.

CRACK! The cat landed

and George's nest began to fall.

"Don't worry,
Mum. I'm all right,"
shouted George.

Down, down, down, he fell.

Twig by twig, the nest fell apart

until only George was left!

"Mum!"

cried George.

"I've lost my nest!"

"George, you have
to flap your wings,"
shouted his mum.
"Now! It's time."

George tried
really hard.

"You can do it,"
said his mum.
"I'm trying,"
said George, and
with a deep breath
and a huge beat
of his wings ...

George flew!

"I knew you could do it, George,"
said his mum.

"I'm ready to fly south now!"
said George. "Let's go! I hope
there's lots of worms…"